TOOTSIE TANNER, WHY DON'T YOU TALK?

OTHER YEARLING BOOKS YOU WILL ENJOY:

YEARLING BOOKS/YOUNG YEARLINGS/YEARLING CLASSICS are designed especially to entertain and enlighten young people. Patricia Reilly Giff, consultant to this series, received the bachelor's degree from Marymount College. She holds the master's degree in history from St. John's University, and a Professional Diploma in Reading from Hofstra University. She was a teacher and reading consultant for many years, and is the author of numerous books for young readers.

For a complete listing of all Yearling titles,
write to Dell Readers Service,
P.O. Box 1045, South Holland, IL 60473.

TOOTSIE TANNER, WHY DON'T YOU TALK?

PATRICIA REILLY GIFF
Illustrated by ANTHONY KRAMER

A Yearling Book

Published by
Dell Publishing
a division of
Bantam Doubleday Dell Publishing Group, Inc.
666 Fifth Avenue
New York, New York 10103

ISBN: 0-440-40239-5

Reprinted by arrangement with Delacorte Press

Printed in the United States of America

February 1990

10 9 8 7 6 5 4 3 2 1

OPM

With love
to
Tootsie and Jim Giff's children:
Helen Flammer,
Peggy and Jim Gorman,
Mary and Marty Giff,
Agnes and Joe Quirk,
my own Jim,
and in memory of George Flammer

Wed. Oct. 27. Late as a gate.

Tmorrow last day school for week. Tchr conference Fri. YAY and YAHOODIE.

HALLOWEEN on Sun.

Things to do:
1. K.K. Hall. prty Sun. (gt. cstme.)
2. See Detective Garcia for more tips on solving crime.
3. FIND MYSTRY . . . . murder kind.
   strangler
   knifer
   How?
   lk in nwspaper.
4. Solve crime.

CHAPTER 1

Abby Jones was the last one finished. She shoved her social studies book into her desk, jammed her assignment pad in on top of it, then dropped her math test on the teacher's desk.

Mrs. Angrees looked up from her plan book absently. "Have a happy Halloween."

Abby nodded. "You too." She hurried across the room to the door, remembering not to run—Mrs. Angrees was sure death on runners—then raced down the hall. Her best friend, Potsie Torres, would be waiting for her.

"Yahoo," Abby shouted when she saw Potsie sitting on the schoolyard steps.

"Nice to know you're alive," Potsie said, fiddling with her pink glass necklace.

"Sorry. I just couldn't get the answer to that last question."

They started across the schoolyard, jumping back

as a boy dribbling a basketball darted in front of them.

"Weirdos all over the place," Abby complained to Potsie. She raised her voice. "Watch out, noodle-head."

"Watch out yourself, spaghetti brain," he yelled back.

She and Potsie went out the gates and sank down on the apartment-house steps next to the school.

Abby took a deep breath. "Free. No school until Monday."

"Almost free," Potsie said. "We have all that home-work."

"Never mind that now," Abby said. "Sunday is soon enough to think about that junk." She pulled out a newspaper that had been bunched up inside her jeans pocket. "Right now we're going to look for a little murder to solve."

"Not another mystery," Potsie said. "I'm sick of spending half my life afraid."

Abby grinned and began to read. "Nothing. Not one killing. Not even a little shooting."

"Good," said Potsie. "I won't have to lock my window tonight."

"I wouldn't be that sure," Abby said. She turned the paper over. "All anyone is interested in is politics. Boringest stuff."

The weirdo boy from the schoolyard ran up the steps bouncing the basketball between her and Pot-sie.

"Watch where you're going," Abby told him.

"Get off the steps, you two," he said. "You don't even live here."

He banged the palm of his hand against the buzzer, bounced the basketball twice before the buzzer sounded again, then darted inside.

"What a nut case," Potsie said, as they watched the door close behind him.

Abby shook her head, turning the page of the newspaper. "Here's something. It's not quite what I was hoping for, but . . . listen."

SUSPECTED SPY SOUGHT IN SECRETS SALE
André Lemonofsky is wanted for questioning in connection with a roll of missing film which he was supposed to have delivered to Anson Air Force Base. The authorities claim that the film, which is vital to U.S. defense, might have been sold to a foreign power. Lemonofsky was last seen at 214 Washington Avenue at the apartment of Olga Lemonofsky several days ago.

"So?" Potsie asked.

"Washington Avenue, Pots. It's almost on top of us. Three blocks from school, four from home."

Potsie closed her eyes. "Forget it, Abby. Just forget it. I'm not going to get involved in any—"

"Spies," Abby said. "Foreign powers. Did you see that movie on television last night? Killings all over the place. The spy ended up—"

Potsie, eyes still closed, clutched her throat. "I

know. Hanging by his heels from the Statue of Liberty. Disgusting. Absolutely dis—"

Abby leaned forward. "Open your eyes. We're going to take a little walk around the corner to 214 Washington Avenue and see what's going on."

Potsie opened one eye. "I'm afraid."

"You're always afraid. Doesn't mean a thing. We might get this crime solved by the end of the weekend, get our name in the paper, win a medal from the President. Who knows what all might happen?"

Potsie sighed and stood up. "Tomorrow. I have piano lessons four minutes ago."

Abby stared at her. "You're just saying that."

"No, I'm not. It's Thursday, remember? It's three-thirty, remember?"

Abby sighed. "Go ahead. You'll be sorry to miss all this spy stuff." She watched Potsie go up the block. Then she jumped off the steps and hopped over a garbage can. A window opened on the second floor. The weirdo kid shouted down, "So long, stoop-o."

Abby crossed her eyes at him and dashed across the street before the traffic light could turn red.

Washington Avenue. She took a deep breath. Pino's Pizzeria on the corner smelled wonderful. So did Karamel Kandy next door. She stopped for a minute to watch the man in the window. With both hands he was dipping apples into a vat of chocolate, then rolling them in nuts. Her mouth watered. Too bad she didn't have any money with her.

Around her people hurried out of Grand Union, arms loaded with groceries. She moved around them and passed Monster's Hideaway, the costume store, reminding herself to come back in the morning to pick out a stupendous costume.

Two fourteen Washington Avenue was halfway up the block. She stepped into the street and craned her neck to get a good look. It was a so-so building of about fourteen or fifteen stories, probably old as the hills. A taxi horn blared, and she jumped back on the curb again.

She marched up to the lobby door and knocked on the glass.

The doorman was sitting on a stool, his legs wrapped around the rungs. He looked up from his paper, yawning. "Help you?"

"I'm here to see"—she ducked her head—"Marshippp Memmimm. . . ." Her voice trailed off.

"Who?"

"Apartment ten A."

He raised one eyebrow, yawned again, and pressed the buzzer.

She skipped through, and dashed to the elevator before he could change his mind. As the doors opened, a toddler barreled out, her face covered with chocolate. "Gimmie more, Nana," she yelled to the woman who was holding her hand.

The woman looked worn out. Her pink hat was tilted over one ear and her glasses were sliding down her nose.

"Candee," screeched the baby.

"In a minute." The woman panted. "You just have to wait a—"

"Can you help me?" Abby asked. "I'm looking for someone, a woman—"

"Nana, want some shoko—"

"Chocolate," the woman corrected the baby absently.

"A woman with an accent," Abby said.

"Need some choco—"

"You ate it all," said the woman, "every single bit." She looked at Abby. "What did you say, dear? So hard to hear with Lulu carrying on."

"Lulu?"

"Louise."

Abby nodded. "Anyway, I'm looking for—"

"Nana!" Lulu shouted.

"Never mind," Abby said, waving her hand. She stepped into the elevator as the doors began to close.

Abby looked at the board with the numbers. She had been right. Fourteen floors. Olga could be on any one of them. "Eeny, meeny." She shut her eyes and pressed.

The number *eight* lit up on the panel and the elevator started to go up.

When it slid to a stop, she took a breath and hurried out. The hall was long, with spinach-colored walls and eggplant rugs.

She turned to the right and knocked at the first door.

No answer.

She tried the next one, 8G. Someone was talking inside. Someone with an accent? She leaned closer.

The door swung open.

"Yeah?" The woman wore a purple-and-green sweater. She almost matched the hall, Abby thought.

"I'm looking for my aunt," Abby said. "Aunt Olga."

The woman shook her head.

"She has an accent."

"What kind?"

"Any kind. Like a spy, sort of."

The woman looked up at the ceiling. "Why don't you ask Paul, the doorman?"

"He's a little cranky today," Abby said. "I had to ask him something last time and—"

The woman pointed at the floor. "Downstairs. There's someone there. She has an accent. Dark hair all pulled back. Gorgeous."

Abby nodded. "That's probably my aunt." She pushed the stairway door open and raced down to the next floor.

"Seven E," the woman called after her.

Abby opened the door to the next floor as quietly as she could and tiptoed along the carpet. She stopped at the dark-green door of 7E and leaned forward listening.

Inside a woman was on the telephone. She sounded like a spy, mysterious with a deep rolling voice, but she was speaking too softly for Abby to understand the words.

From the corner of her eye she noticed something on the floor a little way from the door, a pink paper or envelope. She had the feeling, too, that someone was watching her. She darted a quick look over her shoulder but the hall seemed empty.

She felt a little prickle of fear between her shoulder blades. She stood there for a moment, but everything was quiet. The only sound was the woman in the apartment speaking softly.

As Abby knelt down on the carpet to pick up the pink paper, she felt something, a vibration.

Footsteps were coming toward her fast.

She looked up. A figure barreled down the hallway toward her . . . someone with wild black curly hair and huge blue eyes.

Before Abby could move, the figure was on her, reaching, grabbing for the paper.

Abby gripped the corner of it as tightly as she could, but the figure, a girl, was stronger. She wrenched the paper out of Abby's hand. Then she shoved her hard.

Abby went down on the floor, banging into the dark-green door.

In a moment the girl was gone, the stairway door closing silently behind her.

Abby was left with a tiny scrap of pink paper between her thumb and middle finger.

Slowly she sat up, rubbing a friction burn on the inside of her wrist.

The door to the apartment opened.

FROM THE MEMO OF ABBY JONES,
SPY SEEKER

Thurs nt. befr supper.

CRIME IN PROGRESS:
1. ***SAW SPY***
    (At least saw his wfe.)
        Olga
    lks like mvie star
    sounds like spy
    (I tld her I was visiting aunt on 10th floor and mixed
    up numbers. She believed. Some spy!)
2. ***WRESTLED WITH GIGANTIC KILLER KID***
3. ***HAVE SKINNY LITTLE PIECE OF PINK PAPER***
        (evidence—save)
            says DDAGH
                (crazy language)

CHAPTER 2

Abby speared the last bite of her pork chop with her fork, dipped it in her applesauce, and shoved it into her mouth.

"Gross," said her brother Dan.

Abby scraped back her chair. "What's gross is having to eat my supper and look at you at the same time."

"You're both gross," Abby's mother said, grinning a little. "Your turn to do the dishes, Abby."

"It's Dan's—"

"Like fun it is," Dan said. "I did them last night. Macaroni and cheese. Orange goop all stuck to the plates. Especially yours."

Abby held up her hand. "Don't talk about it. I can't stand that stuff." She shuddered, then reached for her father's plate, slid her own on top of it, and went into the kitchen.

Ten minutes later, she shoved the last dish into the dishwasher. Grabbing her jeans jacket, she started down the hall. "Going around the corner with Potsie," she called.

"You're going to let that kid out in the dark?" she heard Dan ask.

"Mind your own business," she yelled back. "There are about a million people on the street. Busy as anything."

"Where are you going, Abby?" her father asked.

"To the station house. We have to see Detective Garcia."

"They must think you're some kind of pest," Dan said.

"They do not." Her old friend Garcia liked it when she and Potsie came around. He had even helped them solve two mysteries. Witkowski was another story. She frowned, thinking about Garcia's partner.

Witkowski, with his pumpkin-colored hair and his two million cups of coffee a day, thought she was a pain in the neck, all right. He was always trying to get rid of her.

"Be back in an hour, then," her father said.

Abby let herself out the apartment door and went down the corridor to the stairway, passing the elevator.

She tried to keep out of the elevator as much as she could. It was old and creaky, and one of these days it was going to crash right through to the basement.

She took the stairs two at a time, then crossed the street looking up at Potsie's apartment. Potsie stuck her head out the window. "Two minutes," she yelled.

Abby leaned back against the building. It smelled

like fall outside, cool and crisp. Mr. Tannenbaum had put a huge jack-o'-lantern in his candy-store window, and the A&P was decorated with red and yellow leaves and piles of apples in the window.

Potsie raced out the door, breathless. "Had to change," she said. "Shorts were too cool, my mother said. Probably going to die in these sweats."

"Sweats, smeats," Abby said. "Don't waste any more time. I've only got an hour."

They started down the street.

"Find the spy?" Potsie asked.

"Of course," Abby said. "Now we just have to nail her somehow."

"Him, you mean."

"Right." They went around to the back of the station house and climbed onto a pile of old rubber tires to peer in the window.

Garcia was sitting at a desk typing with two fingers. He was wearing an old green shirt and had a pencil stuck behind one ear.

Next to Garcia sat Witkowski, feet up, cup of coffee in his hand, talking with someone on the phone.

Witkowski was always on the phone.

Abby tapped on the window pane a couple of times until Garcia swiveled around and grinned at her. "Come on around to the front," he said. "I'm not doing a thing but writing up some old cases."

They skipped around to the big green doors, quickly passed the sergeant at the desk, and opened the door to the detective squad room.

Witkowski looked up at her, raising his bushy orange eyebrows and shaking his head. "What a way to begin my tour."

Garcia patted the chair next to his desk. "Sit down, Abby. You, too, Potsie. Don't pay any attention to him. He's even more miserable than usual because we can't solve our runaway case."

"Runaway?" Abby reached for her red memo pad. "What's his name? Where—"

Witkowski threw his hands up in the air. "Don't even think of it. The last thing I need is you breathing over my shoulder, gumming up the works."

Abby swiveled around in the chair so she wouldn't have to look at him. "I want to ask you something," she told Garcia.

Garcia leaned back in his seat. "Anything. Ask away."

"Well, suppose you had a case—"

"How could he get to solve it with someone hanging around, asking a million questions?" Witkowski said, rattling his newspaper.

Garcia smiled at her, crinkling his brown eyes. "I told you, Abby. Don't pay any attention."

"I'm not," she said. "I wanted to ask you some stuff about solving a crime. Let's say you wanted to find somebody and somebody else saw this person but—"

"Sounds like the runaway case," Garcia said.

"No." Abby shook her head. "It's something else, really. Spy stuff."

"I'm relieved to hear it," said Witkowski. "We leave the spies to the FBI."

"Good idea," said Potsie.

Garcia opened his desk drawer and took out a bag of Big Baby butterscotch bars. "Help yourself," he said.

Abby took one and pushed the bag over to Potsie. "Got any tips for us?" she asked.

"I saw something today," Garcia said. "It was really great. A man saw a crime . . . a robbery. The robber jumped into a car and—"

"Didn't the man get the license plate number?" She popped another piece of butterscotch into her mouth and pushed the bag back to him.

He reached for it. "That's the thing. He said he saw the license plate, but the car moved away so fast he forgot."

"I would have remembered," Abby said. "I would have raced up behind it—"

"I would have run the other way," Potsie said.

Garcia laughed. "Anyway, we brought in a police-department hypnotist."

Abby leaned forward. "I didn't know there was such a thing."

Garcia nodded. "The hypnotist helped the man remember. He had a little glass ball on a chain, swung it back and forth, told the man to relax . . ."

"Hypnotized?" Abby tucked her leg underneath her. "You mean like . . . you're getting sleeepy. . . ."

Garcia closed his eyes and made a snoring noise.

"Good grief," Witkowski said. "They'll be trying to turn me into a chicken next."

Garcia opened his eyes. "No, actually," he said, his

15

cheek bulging, "the hypnotist told the man to picture the car backing up, coming closer until he could
see the plates clearly—" He broke off and put his
hand up to his mouth. "These butterscotch things
could tear the teeth right out of your head."

Potsie nodded. "That's what my dentist said."

"Anyway," Garcia said, "the man told us the plate
number XL 187. We found the car, arrested the robber . . ." He snapped his fingers. "Case closed. Another winner for Jim Garcia."

Just then the door to the squad room banged
opened. The sergeant stuck his head in. "Got to roll,
guys. Got a case for you."

Witkowski stood up. "Never will finish this paper."
He reached across the desk and grabbed a butterscotch bar.

"I guess we can't come," Abby said.

"Sorry, honey," Garcia said. "Another couple of
years. You'll make sergeant by the time you're six-
teen."

A moment later they were gone.

Abby stood up. The leg she had been sitting on felt
numb with pins and needles.

She hated that feeling.

"Come on, Potsie," she said. They wandered out of
the station house. "Maybe we could use hypnotism to
solve this spy case."

"Don't even think about it," Potsie said. "I don't
want to hear the word *spy*. It makes me shiver."

"I'll have to get hold of a little ball on a chain
tomorrow. Just in case. Maybe when we go to the

costume store for our Halloween stuff." Abby grinned. "Too bad we really couldn't turn Witkowski into a chicken. Serve him right up for dinner, maybe to that weirdo kid we saw today."

She looked around. It was getting late. The street wasn't nearly as busy as it had been an hour ago.

An hour. "Potsie," she said, "how long since we left home?"

"Maybe we should be getting home," Potsie said. "It's really getting late."

They started to hurry. As they turned the corner, Abby spotted someone in front of them. Someone familiar.

She wrinkled her forehead, trying to remember who it was.

A girl with dark curly hair. Very dark, and tall.

Abby felt a strange feeling, a feeling of fear. She stiffened. She knew who it was.

It was the giant killer kid.

She grabbed Potsie's arm and dragged her into Mr. Tannenbaum's doorway to peek out from behind the jack-o'-lantern.

The girl with the dark curly hair rushed down Washington Avenue.

CHAPTER 3

"Who?" Potsie asked. "What—"

"Ssh." Abby could feel her heart pounding. She took a deep breath and tried to remember all the things Garcia had told her about following people, or tailing them, as he called it.

"Hey," Mr. Tannenbaum called to them. "Are you coming in or what? I'm waiting to close up."

Abby shook her head. "Not tonight. We're just watching, waiting for . . ."

"Who?" Potsie asked again.

The girl turned the corner.

"Come on, Potsie, let's go."

Potsie stuck out her bottom lip. "I'm not moving one inch until you tell me what this is all about."

Abby gritted her teeth. "We're going to lose her."

"Not one inch."

"All right. She was in the spy's apartment house. She knocked me over—" Abby broke off. "Let's go."

"Suppose she sees us," Potsie said. "Suppose—"

"Don't worry, she won't." Abby grabbed Potsie's arm and started to run.

Too bad she had on her clunky shoes instead of sneakers, she thought. Too bad her mother had said they were too expensive to throw out. Nobody had shoes like that anymore. Besides they made more noise than the garbage truck that woke her up every morning.

They turned the corner. For a moment she couldn't see the girl. "Where . . ." She spotted her crossing L Street between a motorcycle and a navy Toyota.

She drew in her breath. "Look, Pots, there's the weirdo boy. It looks as if he's sneaking around, following her too."

"I can't keep up." Potsie gasped. She sank down on a doorstep.

Abby tore after the girl alone, trying to run on tiptoes. She dived across the street behind the motorcycle and felt her jacket catch on something. She could feel herself falling. She went down on the street hard, the wind knocked out of her.

Ahead of her the girl turned. Abby looked up at her.

The girl started back across the street toward her.

Frantically Abby began to scramble to her feet. "Potsie?" she yelled as loud as she could.

"Can I help you?" the girl called.

"Stay away from me," Abby yelled. "I'm a judo expert."

"Hey," said the girl. "I was only trying to help. Bunch of crazies in this city, if you ask me."

Abby dusted off her knees. "You're right. Crazies who bother people in hallways. . . ." She backed away from the girl. "Crazies like you."

"Me? I never saw you before in my life."

"Don't tell me that," Abby said, outraged. She held out her wrist. "Look at this friction burn I got on that purple rug. All because of you."

An odd look crossed the girl's face. She took a deep breath. Her huge blue eyes looked sympathetic. "Oh, no," she said. "Tootsie Tanner again, I'll bet anything."

Potsie came running up. "Should I call the police?"

"I'm all right." Abby waved her hand. "Tootsie who?" she asked the girl.

The girl put her hands on her hips. Her nails were long, and each one was painted a different color. "Tanner," she said absently. "She looked like me, right?"

"Exactly."

The girl shook her head. "No, not exactly." She touched the front of her neck with one blue-tipped finger. "She has this little mole, right here. She wears scarves to cover it up."

"You could be twins," Abby said.

"We are twins," said the girl. "I'm Tillie. Tillie Tanner."

Tillie sighed. "Tootsie's mean, meaner than a snake. She sees something she wants—snap, bam— she goes after it, and you'd better watch out, baby."

She pointed a crimson nail at Abby, then flicked her fingers at Potsie. "Neat, huh? I'm a nail freak. Love the way they look."

Abby nodded. "You and Tootsie live in that apartment? Two fourteen Washington Avenue?"

"The one with the yuck green walls and purple rugs? Don't be ridiculous. I wouldn't be caught dead living in a place like that—" She broke off. "Listen, I've got some money. How about a yogurt or something?"

"We're late," Potsie said. "Really late."

Abby thought for a moment. Her hour must certainly be up by now. But this might be her only chance to find out about Tootsie. She must have something to do with that spy, otherwise why had she taken that pink paper? Why had she even been in that building? "I've got about ten minutes," Abby said. "Ten minutes at the most."

"I've got zilch," Potsie said. "I've got to go home."

"You're sure?"

Potsie nodded. "Sure. See you tomorrow." She smiled at Abby and headed for home.

Abby dusted off her jeans again, then headed for Yahoo Yogurt with Tillie.

"Hey," she said. "I just thought. The weirdo boy."

"Sam? You mean Sam?"

"He was following you around."

Tillie rolled her eyes. "He's crazy about me. Follows me everywhere. Does what I want." She smiled. "Boys are always crazy about me."

Abby bit at her fingernail. Wait till she told Potsie. Potsie would laugh like anything.

They turned in at Yahoo Yogurt. Inside the place was painted in yellow stripes. A sign read: YELL FOR YELLOW YOGURT.

They waited in line. "I'm going to have a banana delight," Tillie said. "It's got nuts and a whole bunch of other stuff. I'm starved."

"I guess I'll have strawberry," Abby said. "But listen, I wanted to ask you about Tootsie. How come she was running around in two fourteen Washington Avenue if she doesn't live there?"

"Banana delight," Tillie told the counterman. "Make it vanilla, double scoop, and double on the almonds, too, okay? Make it an extra banana too."

"Extra nickel for the almonds," he said. "Dime for the banana slice."

She waved her hand around. "Double strawberry for my friend too." She turned to Abby. "What's your name, anyway?"

The man handed them a tray with two yogurt dishes piled high. "Pay the cashier." He handed Tillie a yellow slip.

"Abby," Abby said. "But listen, how come—"

Ahead of her Tillie slid into a booth and took a huge bite of the banana. "Running. Tootsie's a runner. Runs up and down the avenue, into apartment buildings, airports, railway stations . . ."

"Airports?"

"Well, you know what I mean. She's training, wants to win the Olympics, or something. Relay racing, that's Tootsie's strong point. That's probably why she took that paper away from you."

Tillie flicked an almond off the side of her face with a lilac-colored nail. "Is that where you live? On Washington Avenue?"

Abby shook her head, mouth full.

"You a runner too?" Tillie asked.

She swallowed. "Uh-uh."

"Then what—"

"I was looking for someone."

"Who?"

"A friend," Abby said, hunching herself over her yogurt uneasily.

Tillie held her cup up in the air and drained the last of the melted yogurt. "Listen, kid, I've got to go." She slapped her pockets. "What do you know? I forgot my wallet. How about you pay this time, I'll get it next."

Abby reached into her jacket pocket. "I'm not sure . . ."

"Dig deep, kid."

Abby looked up at her. "Yes. Couple of dollars right here."

Tillie stood up.

"Wait a minute," Abby said, trying to think of what else to ask her. "Where do you live, anyway?"

"Tell you what, tomorrow's Saturday. I'll meet you on Washington Avenue somewhere. We can look for your friend together. What did you say her name was?"

"Olga," Abby said before she could think.

"In front of Tannenbaum's?"

Abby nodded. "Fine, sure."

The girl ran her fingers through her hair. "See you then."

"What time?" Abby yelled after her.

The girl turned. "Noon," she called. She pulled the door open and slammed it shut behind her.

Abby scraped the nuts off the top of her yogurt and pushed it away from her. Yuck stuff. She stood up and headed for the cashier. Suddenly she thought about the time. It was probably after ten. Her father would have a fit.

She felt like having a fit too. It had taken her weeks to save the money for a spectacular costume. Now a bunch of money was down the drain.

She put the two dollars down on the green rubber pad and hurried out the door.

It wasn't until she turned up L Street that she began to think about some of the things Tillie had said.

There was something wrong. Something . . . She couldn't put her finger on what it was.

She tore up the stairs to her apartment and let herself in. She had to call Potsie and fill her in on all the news.

FROM THE MEMO OF ABBY JONES
SUPER SLEUTH

Fri. morn. early

Thngs to do:

Go to Monster's Hide a way:

1. Buy cstme for K.K.'s Halloween prty.
2. Buy 1 ball and chain for hyp.

Prctice hyp.

Meet Tillie Tanner at Tannenbaum's tomorrow.****

PROGRESS IN CRME:

N*O*T*H*I*N*G N*E*W*.

DO SOMETHING DRDFUL TO DAN FOR TLLING ON ME GET. HOME LTE WHEN M&D GOT HME FROM MOVIE LAST NT.

CHAPTER 4

Abby and Potsie stopped for a minute to look in the window of Slummer's Bakery Store. A bunch of orange iced crullers were piled high in front.

"If only I hadn't spent so much on yogurt last night," Abby said.

"Never mind," said Potsie. "Those crullers are almost as bad for your teeth as butterscotch bars. I know. I had fourteen cavities last time I went to the dentist."

"You're right. Besides, we don't want to waste any more time. All the best costumes will be gone."

They turned the corner and headed for Washington Avenue.

The man in Karamel Kandy was pouring pink syrup over a tray of mints.

"That's a sickly-looking pink," Potsie said. "Looks like the medicine I took the last time I had a stomach-ache."

Abby stopped to stare at the syrup. It reminded her of something.

What was it?

It was something that reminded her of Tillie, something that had bothered her last night too.

She closed her eyes. "Syrup," she muttered under her breath. "Pink syrup."

She opened her eyes to see Potsie staring at her. "I haven't gone crazy," she said. "I'm just trying to think . . . just . . ."

By the time they reached Monster's Hideaway she realized what it was. "The pink paper," she said. "The paper Tootsie snatched out of my hand."

"What—?"

"How did Tillie know about it?" Abby thought back to the Yahoo Yogurt place, Tillie sitting with a mouthful of banana, saying something about Tootsie wanting to win the Olympics and that was why she had grabbed the paper. "What nonsense," Abby muttered. "I should have picked that up sooner."

Potsie raised one shoulder.

"As soon as we get finished at the costume place, I'm going to head right over to Tannenbaum's, wait there all day if I have to, find out just what's going on with the Tanner twins."

Potsie sighed. "Can't we just enjoy Halloween weekend? Do we have to go on all these wild goose chases?"

"We're going to get to the bottom of this," Abby said firmly.

They turned into Monster's Hideaway. It was a mess of counters piled high with masks and costumes. In front a fat lady was trying on a blue angel costume. The wings looked like little peanuts stretched across her back.

"I'm going to take a look at some gorilla stuff," Potsie said. "See you in a few minutes."

Abby nodded. She started for the cashier's counter, and nearly tripped over a tall skinny man in a baby's bonnet. He had a pink pacifier in his hand.

"Excuse me," Abby said to the cashier, "I need a ball on a chain."

The woman pointed toward the back. "Last aisle, prisoner costumes."

Abby shook her head. "Not that kind."

"Magician's? Crystal ball?"

"No. It has to have a string attached."

The woman raised her eyes to the ceiling. "I'm a little busy right now or haven't you noticed? About a thousand people in here looking for all kinds of oddball stuff."

"It's for hypnotism."

"I'm probably all out of it."

"I guess I'll look at the magicians' stuff," Abby said.

"Near the windows to the right."

Abby hurried toward the front and pawed through the things on the counter. There were about a million crystal balls . . . one as big as her head, some medium sized ones . . . and underneath a small clear one on a long gold chain.

Terrific. She picked it up and walked toward the back, swinging it in her hand. If she could find some kind of a spiffy costume she'd be out of here in ten minutes, ready to meet Tillie Tanner. She looked back to see what Potsie was doing. She could see a big gorilla head and Potsie's skinny legs poking out the bottom.

She picked up a gold sequined hat, put it down, then tried on a Red Riding Hood cape.

If only she knew what she wanted to be.

Last year she had looked like a complete nerd dressed in a black cat suit. The tail had fallen off about a dozen times.

She walked toward the back, put on a pair of gold tinted glasses, and looked at herself in the round mirror on the wall.

In back of her the door opened. She looked into the mirror. A woman was walking in, heading toward her.

It was Olga Lemonofsky.

Abby dropped the glasses back on the counter. She moved down the aisle a little way, maneuvering around two kids who were trying on bald-man wigs.

She ducked behind a counter and reached up for a mask that would cover her face. The first one she touched felt like rubber. Still kneeling, she pulled it on, then stood up and took a quick look in the mirror.

A black cat with stand up ears and an iridescent nose stared back at her.

She wondered who would buy such an ugly thing.

Then she had to grin behind her whiskers. It was the same mask she had bought last year.

She sauntered up the aisle past the kids, and made her way to Olga Lemonofsky.

Olga was wearing a bright blue dress with beads. She was looking at a ballerina outfit . . . one of those pink things with a poufy net skirt.

She had some nerve, Abby thought. Even though she had a gorgeous face, she was probably twenty-five years old. Much too old for that kind of stuff.

Abby realized her hands were free. She looked down. Where was the ball and chain? She glanced over her shoulder. She must have dropped it on the counter when she put on the cat mask. She'd have to go back for it. Maybe she could hypnotize Olga Lemonofsky right now. Find out about her husband, and solve the crime before the day was over.

Just then Olga looked up. "What do you think of this?" she asked.

If only she had the ball and chain in her hand, she thought.

"I would wear it with a little silver tiara," Olga said.

Abby nodded, listening to her accent. It sounded terrific. She wished she could talk like that.

"Or maybe a gold one," Olga said.

"Mmm," said Abby. It was hard to breathe behind the mask, hard to speak.

"You think so?"

"How about something with more to it?" Abby said in a muffled voice.

"Excuse me?"

31

"Slacks, or something. Cover your legs."

Behind her something growled.

Potsie's imitation of a gorilla.

With one hand behind her back Abby waved her away.

Potsie snarled.

The door to the store opened. A bunch of kids came in laughing and pushing each other.

"Excuse me," Abby said. "I'll be back in half a second."

She raced back to the cat counter and began to look for the ball and chain.

It wasn't there. It wasn't on the floor either. She spotted one of the kids who had been trying on bald-man wigs. The kid was waving the glass ball around in front of her friend.

"Hey, that's mine," Abby said.

"Finders keepers," said the kid.

"No good," said Abby, hand out.

"Give it to her," the other kid said. "It's a piece of junk anyway."

Abby grabbed the ball and chain and raced back to where she had left Olga Lemonofsky.

Olga was gone.

Still in her gorilla mask, Potsie was holding up the ballerina costume with two fingers.

"Where'd she go?" Abby asked.

"Who?"

"The woman who just had that costume."

"The gorgeous . . . ?"

"She's the spy, Pots. The one from the apartment house up the street."

Potsie dropped the costume back on the counter and stared at it. She wiped her hands on her jeans. "I can't believe it," she said. "A real live spy."

CHAPTER 5

Tillie was late. Abby shifted from one foot to the other in front of Tannenbaum's Candy Store. She was disgusted. Half of Saturday was gone, and nothing was done.

She hadn't even bought a costume. Potsie had plunked down five dollars for that silly gorilla head, but she hadn't found a thing . . . even though she had tried on everything in sight.

If only she had had time to hypnotize Olga. She might have found out where André Lemonofsky was, she might even have found out about the film.

She wished Potsie hadn't rushed home to try on the gorilla head. It was boring standing there by herself. Just when she was about to give up and head over to 214 Washington Avenue for a little spying, Tillie rounded the corner.

"I've been standing here so long, I'm ready to be planted," Abby said.

"I rushed as fast as I could," Tillie said. "I had to do

my nails . . . Purple Witchery. . . . I didn't even get to have any lunch."

"Me neither," Abby said. "We could get something right now. A little candy in Tannenbaum's."

"I don't have any . . ." Tillie began. She looked down at her nails.

"Money?" Abby finished for her. "Forgot your wallet again?"

"No." Tillie shook her head. "It's really a terrible story. . . ."

"Look," Abby said. "I still have some money." She thought about her costume. "Not too much."

"Maybe we could go over to Coco's, then," Tillie said. "I'm starving."

Abby reached into her pocket. "A dollar's worth of stuff," she said. "And that's it. Otherwise I won't have enough money for a costume for Kiki Krumback's Halloween party."

"Lucky," Tillie said as they headed for Coco's. "I've never been to a dress-up party like that."

"Kiki's mother takes care of our apartment house," Abby said. "And Kiki hangs around all day eating."

She wondered if Kiki would mind if she asked Tillie to come.

"Do you think your friend would mind if . . ."

"I'll ask," Abby said. "As soon as I get home."

They turned into Coco's and sat on the brown leather stools at the counter.

"Eggs," said Tillie. "Scrambled eggs and bacon."

Abby swallowed. "I guess I'll just have a Coke."

"I ordered too much?" Tillie asked.

"Er . . ." Abby began.

"Make it one egg," Tillie told the waitress. She spread a napkin over her jeans. "Listen," she said. "Abby? That's your name? As soon as I can I'll treat. Just now . . ."

"You're a little broke?"

The waitress slid Abby's Coke on the counter. "Egg will be ready in a minute."

"I'd have money," Tillie said, "if it weren't for Tootsie."

"Tootsie?"

"She's a devil, that sister of mine. Ever since she was a little kid. She sneaks around poking her nose into everyone's business . . . just like what happened in the apartment house with you yesterday. . . ."

"That reminds me," Abby said, taking a sip of her Coke. "How did you know about the paper?"

Tillie examined one of her nails. "What paper?"

Abby stared at her. "The pink paper. Tootsie pulled it out of my hand. You know that, don't you?"

Tillie didn't answer for a moment. She watched the waitress bring her plate, then picked up her knife and fork.

"Tillie," Abby said.

Tillie sighed and ran her hand through her thick black curls. "Listen, I hate to tell you this. I hate to tell anyone." She stopped to take a forkful of scrambled egg. "It's disloyal, really."

Abby leaned a little closer. "I won't tell anyone, I promise."

Tillie waited for a minute, chewing. Then she spoke. "Yes, I knew about the paper. She's bad, that one, bad. Even though she's my sister . . ."

"She's involved with spying?"

Tillie blinked. "Spying? Are you crazy? What are you talking about?"

"Forget it," Abby said. She leaned over her straw, thinking that she had a big mouth, thinking that Garcia would never had made a mistake like that. "We were talking about the pink paper, remember? Tootsie told you about it?"

Tillie crumbled a piece of bacon into her mouth. "Not exactly," she said. "Tootsie doesn't talk."

"Not at all?"

"Not one word, not one syllable. Nothing. Zilch."

"What's the matter with her?"

Tillie raised one shoulder. "Who knows?" She took another bite of her egg.

Abby glanced at the bacon. The smell was driving her crazy. It looked delicious, all crisp and brown. She'd like to reach over and grab—

"Would you like a piece of the bacon?" Tillie asked.

"Well . . ." Abby began.

Tillie shook her head. "Not hungry?" She shoved the bacon into her mouth. "Anyway, about Tootsie. I saw it in her diary."

"The pink paper?"

Tillie shook her head, mouth full. "No, she wrote about what happened. The pink paper was nothing. An advertisement. She just did it because she wanted to." She swallowed. "I told you she was a rip."

"Just an advertisement? Are you sure?" Abby asked.

"Sure as anything. But my wallet, that's the real problem. Tootsie took it. She's not going to give it back either. I can tell you that. It's probably down the tubes somewhere. In a garbage pail. A sewer, maybe." She shrugged. "Who knows?"

Abby looked at her. Her huge blue eyes had misted over. Maybe she was going to cry any minute.

Dan was tough to have around, Abby thought, but he'd never steal her money. She really felt sorry for Tillie.

"What about this spy business?" Tillie asked.

Abby took a last swallow of her Coke. Should she tell Tillie?

Why not?

She scooped a piece of ice out of the glass and put it into her mouth.

"The truth is," she told Tillie, "I'm on a case. Investigating a spy."

Tillie's mouth opened. "At Two fourteen Washington Avenue?"

Abby bit her ice in half. "Exactly."

Tillie wiped up the egg on her plate with a piece of toast. "Well . . ."

"Want to come with me," Abby asked. "I'm hoping she'll be home now."

"What are you going to do?"

"I'm not sure exactly," Abby said. "I have a couple of ideas."

She reached into her pocket, feeling the long gold

chain. If only she did have an idea. She paid the counterman, slid off the stool, and headed for Washington Avenue with Tillie following her.

The doorman was standing outside.

Abby waved at him. "Remember me? Going to see my aunt."

He muttered something, hardly paying attention.

"What's the name of this spy?" Tillie asked when they were in the lobby.

Abby looked around. "Olga." She pressed the elevator button and they stepped inside.

"Seventh floor," she told Tillie.

"Seven what?"

"Seven E."

"Can't be," Tillie said and closed her mouth tight.

"What do you mean? Do you know her?"

Tillie shook her head. "Of course not. I was thinking of something else."

The elevator door slid open. They tiptoed down the purple-carpeted corridor.

Abby watched Tillie out of the corner of her eye. Tillie knew something about Olga Lemonofsky all right. She should never have told her what she was doing.

She wondered if she were in danger, walking down the dark hall with her. Nobody even knew where she was.

Tillie nudged her.

Abby jumped.

"Someone's coming on the other elevator," Tillie whispered.

"I don't hear anything," Abby said.

Then she did hear it, the sound of the elevator motor.

Tillie grabbed her roughly by the arm and pulled her into the emergency stairway.

CHAPTER 6

A small, dusty window faced back onto the green-and-purple corridor. Abby stood up on tiptoe, rubbing her arm, to see who was coming.

"Sorry I yanked on you so hard," Tillie said. "I thought we were going to be caught."

"Nearly tore my arm right out of the socket," Abby muttered. "And it's the same one with the friction burn from Tootsie."

"Sorry," Tillie said again. "I'm really sorry as anything."

"Don't worry," Abby said. "Duck. Here comes somebody." She dived below the window.

She heard someone say something and laugh. The voice had an accent.

It was Olga Lemonofsky, she was sure of it, and she wasn't alone. Abby heard a male voice, too, muffled, indistinct.

It was her husband, the spy. It had to be.

A door closed. Everything was quiet.

She glanced over at Tillie. Tillie was leaning back against the wall, her face white, her eyes huge in her pale face.

"What is it?" she asked Tillie urgently. "What's the matter?"

Tillie shook her head. "It's nothing," she said after a moment. "I just thought we were going to be caught."

"Did you see who it was?"

Tillie hesitated. "Not exactly. A woman. A man was with her."

"Don't be nervous," Abby said. She waved her hand around. "I do this stuff all the time."

"Not me." Tillie ran bright purple nails through her hair. "Let's get out of here."

"Wait a minute. Was the spy wearing a blue dress?"

"Spy?" Tillie cut in. "That wasn't a spy."

"Listen, Tillie. There's one thing you have to learn in this business. Just because someone is good looking doesn't mean she's not a criminal."

Abby sat back against the stairs. Now that she knew André Lemonofsky was in the apartment with Olga, what was she going to do?

She could call the FBI . . . or maybe Garcia.

Yes, Garcia. He'd know what to do.

She stood up. "Come on, Tillie. I've got to make a quick telephone call."

Tillie pushed open the door to the corridor.

"No time for the elevator," Abby said. "We have to take the stairs."

"Seven flights? Are you crazy?"

Abby started down, glad she had worn her sneakers this morning. She felt as if she were flying as her feet skimmed down the stairs.

She reached the outside door long before Tillie and had to wait for her to catch up.

"Who are you going to call?" Tillie asked breathlessly.

"An old friend," Abby said. "I'll explain later."

With Tillie following she rushed around the corner.

A woman was leaning against the telephone, speaking in a loud voice. "I told Mabel about the movie. What movie? Haven't you been listening? It's the best . . ."

Abby moved around so the woman could see she was waiting.

"The very best I've ever—"

Abby tapped her on the shoulder. "This is a police emergency."

"What?" Tillie said.

The woman's eyes widened. "Are you—"

Abby held up her hand. "It's the truth."

The woman slammed the phone down and walked away.

Abby picked it up, still warm from the woman's ear. She dialed the station-house number. "Garcia, please."

"Are you crazy?" Tillie said.

Abby shook her head. "It's not exactly the way it sounds. Don't worry."

"Garcia's not here," the voice said. "How about his partner, Witkowski?"

Just her luck, Abby thought. She wondered if she should tell Witkowski what she had seen. He might not even believe her.

"Miss?"

"Yes. All right. Let me talk to Witkowski." A minute later she heard his gravelly voice.

"It's me," she said.

"Ten million people in this city," Witkowski said, "and I have to get a phone call from you."

"Me, Abby Jones."

"I gathered that."

"Listen, Witkowski," she said. "I have to tell you I just found a spy."

"Really?"

"It's that one in the papers. Two fourteen Washington Avenue."

"Listen, Abby," Witkowski said. "What are you up to?"

"It's too long to explain," she said. "You've got to come, right away. It's really—"

He sighed. "Listen, I'm in the middle of something, Jim isn't here. The phones are ringing off the hooks. . . ."

"Please. You'll see when you get here."

"It'll take me a little while. But I want you out of that building."

Abby put the phone back on the hook. For a moment she stood there thinking. Then she snapped her fingers. "Come on, Tillie."

"Maybe we ought to get something to eat. A soda or—"

"I've got to buy a couple of magazines," Abby said. "I think there's a place across the street."

"Get *Seventeen*," Tillie said. "I haven't seen that one this month."

"Not a chance."

"Why not?"

"It's too much to explain right now," Abby said. She began to cross the street.

Tillie followed after her. "How about *Mademoiselle*?"

"Worse yet," Abby said. She hurried into the store and started to thumb through a magazine. "The trouble is I don't really know what spies like to read."

"Detective stuff, I guess," Tillie said. "Suspense."

"Maybe." Abby reached up to the top shelf. "How about *True Confessions*?"

"How about leaving the magazines alone unless you're going to pay for them?" said the man at the counter.

"Of course I'm going to pay." Abby dug into her pocket, pulled out more of her costume money, and tucked a couple of magazines under her arm.

Once she was outside, she stopped to lean against the telephone pole. "Now, here's the way we'll do it," she told Tillie. "We'll ring the bell, hold out the magazines, and see if she wants to buy."

"Who?"

"The spy," Abby said patiently. "Who do you

think? It's going to take Witkowski forever to get here."

"Who's Wit—"

"Never mind. Let's just get going."

Tillie pointed a purple finger at the apartment house. "You mean back up there? No good, no way."

"I'm going right now," Abby said.

"I've got to go home," Tillie said. "This minute. Really. I just thought of something I've got to do right now."

"But . . ." Abby began.

"It won't wait."

Abby watched her rush down the street. What was the matter with that girl, anyway? First she wanted to be a detective, then she chickened out before she even got into the whole thing.

She marched into the apartment building.

"You here again?" the doorman asked, yawning.

"I try to come to see my aunt as much as I can. Every day at least."

She skipped past him into the lobby, then waited at the elevator. Her mouth felt dry. What she was doing was dangerous, she told herself.

The elevator door opened. She took a deep breath, stepped inside, and pressed the button for seven.

Fri Aft. 3:00

TERRBLE THNG

HORRBLE

CAN'T TALK ABT.
CAN'T WRITE ABT.
CAN'T EVEN THNK ABT.

CHAPTER 7

It was late. Abby pushed her memo book away from her. She plumped up her pillow and leaned back against it, reaching for a box of tissues.

She thought back to this afternoon and the ride up in the elevator. She had wondered how long it would take Witkowski to get to 214 Washington Avenue.

She rubbed her eyes with a tissue, wondering if Witkowski had ever gotten there. She was glad that he didn't know the apartment number, glad that . . .

She shut her eyes, remembering what had happened.

She had headed straight for apartment seven E, listened to the sound of voices, and before she could change her mind, pressed the doorbell.

A moment later the door swung open. Olga smiled at her, fingering pale blue beads.

"I'm selling magazines," Abby said, trying to see around her into the living room.

"I see," Olga said. "You are a hardworking girl, right?"

Abby nodded. "Would you like to buy one?" She held out the magazine.

Olga bent down to look. "Detective stories? Suspense?" She wrinkled her nose. "How about some glamor magazines? I like that kind of thing."

"Not right now," Abby said. "But I could get some for you, right away. I'll just leave these in your living room and—"

Olga shook her head. "No, it is too much bother for you. Besides, I'm not alone right now."

"I don't see anyone," Abby said, standing on tiptoes a little. All she could see were a couple of blue-striped chairs and a flowered couch.

"He's in the kitchen," Olga said, still smiling at her.

"Maybe he'd like to buy a magazine."

"I don't think so, but thanks anyway." Olga began to close the door.

Abby patted her jeans pockets. She could feel the long gold chain with the ball on the end. She reached for it. She'd have to use it to find something out, to delay things a little, long enough for Witkowski to get there. He'd be able to arrest the spy before he came out of the kitchen and went somewhere else to do his spying.

She pulled out the ball and chain. It slithered out of her hands and onto the rug.

"Excuse me." She gulped and bent down for it.

"Pretty," said Olga as she straightened up. "A necklace? Is that for sale too?"

Abby held it high. She wished she could remember what Garcia had said about hypnotism. She swung it back and forth gently. "Who's in the kitchen?" she asked.

"What?" Olga wrinkled her forehead.

Abby tried a deeper voice. "Who's in the kitchen?"

Olga smiled. "Does the doorman know you're wandering around in here?"

"Oh, yes," Abby said. "He knows, all right." She swung the ball and chain a little harder.

"Whatever are you doing?" Olga asked.

Abby heard the elevator stop. She breathed a sigh of relief. It certainly had taken Witkowski long enough to get there. She turned.

It wasn't Witkowski at all. It was Lulu and her grandmother.

Lulu had a green all-day sucker in her mouth. Her hands were coated with sticky green sugar too. "Hey, gimme," she said to Abby, reaching for the glass ball.

Abby backed away, putting it behind her.

Lulu began to scream.

At the same time Olga stuck her head out the door. "How are you today?" she shouted to Lulu's grand-mother.

"Bearing up," the woman said, pushing at her pink hat. "Lulu certainly is a handful."

Lulu circled around in back of Abby, reaching for the magazines.

"Want to buy a magazine?" Olga asked. "This little girl is dying to sell some."

Abby slipped the ball and chain into her pocket as Lulu made another grab for it.

"Magazines?" the woman shouted. "What kind of magazines?"

"Detective," Abby said reluctantly.

"Suspense," said Olga at the same time.

"Perfect," said the woman. "I like to read detective stuff."

"Run along, then," Olga said, patting Abby on the shoulder. "That's a terrific sale for you."

Abby nodded. "I will. How about the ball and chain?"

"What?"

"I mean the necklace." She glanced down at Lulu, who was pulling at her jeans with sticky fingers.

"What about it?"

"It's for sale."

"Let me think about it," Olga said.

Lulu's grandmother held out two dollar bills. "For the magazine," she said.

Abby handed her the magazine. She shoved the money into her pocket as the woman went down the hall, dragging Lulu behind her.

"Whoosh," Olga said. "That's a lot of noise for one little baby."

Abby grinned. Too bad Olga was a spy. She looked too nice to be a criminal.

Olga tapped her on the shoulder again. "Would you like a quick glass of soda?"

Abby took a deep breath. "Sure I would. Great idea."

A door banged shut in the kitchen. "Are we going to have some supper or will I starve to death?" a voice called out.

Olga began to laugh.

Abby took a step backward. She knew that voice. She'd know it anywhere.

"A little girl is here," Olga called. "She's dying of thirst."

"No, listen," Abby began.

"One Coke coming up," said the voice.

"Come in for a minute," Olga said.

Abby took another step down the hall. She had to get out of there right now. "I just remembered something. I have to go home."

"Come and get it," the voice called from the kitchen.

"Just for a minute?" Olga asked.

Abby shook her head. She turned and raced down the hall. She didn't wait for the elevator. Instead she pushed open the door and raced down the stairs.

The voice belonged to Garcia. Garcia, her friend. Garcia, the detective.

Abby shuddered. Garcia, the spy.

Sat. morn.

GARCIA
1. Spy? All this time in P.D. gtting secrets and stuff?
        CAN'T BELIEVE
        NEVER
2. Maybe he's investigating Olga Lemonofsky
        Gt over to station hs. and
        fnd out.
        RIGHT AWAY.

CHAPTER 8

Abby shrugged into her jeans jacket, scooped what was left of her money off the dresser, and went into the kitchen.

"I'll be back in a little while," she told her mother.

Her mother stopped stirring and pushed a strand of hair behind her ear. "I'm making Grandma's chicken soup for dinner. Homemade bread too."

"Wow." Abby stopped for a moment, thinking. "I have a new friend. She likes to eat a lot. If I run into her, can I . . ."

"Why not? I even bought some of those Halloween cupcakes. You know, the orange kind with the scarecrows on top."

"How about Potsie too?"

Her mother nodded and started to stir again.

"Great." Abby bounced a kiss off the side of her mother's head and let herself out the door.

Kiki Krumback was sitting on the steps munching on an apple. She was stuffed into a brown-and-orange striped dress. "Don't forget the Halloween party to-night," she said. "I'm going to give a prize for the kid with the best costume."

Abby nodded. "What's the prize?"

Kiki raised one shoulder. "Who knows? I'll figure it out any minute now."

"Can I bring a friend?" Abby asked. "Two friends. They're twins."

"Are they cute?"

"Don't be silly. They're girls."

Kiki shrugged again. "Why not? Too bad they're not boys. Not counting grown-ups, only two boys are coming so far, and I figure they might back out if they realize."

"Who needs them?" Abby said. She crossed the street to Potsie's apartment house and buzzed for Potsie.

How could she ever tell Potsie that Garcia was a spy?

A few minutes later, Potsie appeared in the lobby. "Where are we going?"

"Over to the station house," Abby said. "We have to find out a few things."

"Like what?"

"Like what Garcia was doing in Olga the spy's apartment yesterday."

Potsie's eyes widened. "You don't think that Garcia . . . you can't think he'd give away secrets to . . ."

Abby closed her mouth tight and shrugged.

"Garcia?" Potsie asked.

They hurried to the station house and went around

58

to stand on the rubber tires. They could see the squad room through the window. Both Garcia and Witkowski were there, Witkowski with the phone cradled on his shoulder, and Garcia hunched over his desk staring at something.

Abby rapped on the dusty window.

Witkowski turned and frowned, but Garcia motioned for them to come around to the front.

On the way Abby rubbed her hands on her jeans. They were damp with perspiration. Garcia wasn't a spy, she told herself. He didn't look like a spy, he didn't act like one.

Suppose he was a spy, a small voice said inside her.

She nearly bumped into a policeman coming out the door. "Sorry," she said. They made a dash for the squad room.

"Hey, you two," yelled the sergeant at the desk.

"Garcia said," Abby called back and pushed open the door.

Garcia tossed a piece of paper into the wastebasket. "Whorls," he muttered. "Double loops."

They went over to his desk. Abby stood at one end, while Potsie slid onto the chair in front. Garcia's curly hair was standing up on end. "Studying fingerprints," he said. "Everyone is different, everyone in the world has his own unique print. But there are three different categories: loops, whorls, and arches."

Abby nodded as he began to draw them.

He looked up. "What's the matter, kids? You look like a pair of Halloween ghosts."

"Nothing," Abby said. She shook her head.

"Not a thing," Potsie said at the same time. "What did you do yesterday?"

Abby glared at her. Potsie should know better, she thought. You couldn't come right out and ask. . . .

"Something's the matter, all right," said Witkowski, putting down the phone. "Calling me like that . . ."

Abby swallowed. She had completely forgotten about that call to Witkowski. How could she? She would never have come barreling over here. She would have waited a few days, given him the chance to forget all about it. "It was a mistake," she told him, glancing away from Garcia's eyes.

"I want to know—" Witkowski began, but the phone rang. He shook his head and reached for it.

Garcia grinned and pushed the second chair over for Abby. "Saved by the bell."

She sat down gingerly. "Did you have an interesting case yesterday?" she asked, thinking she was as bad as Potsie.

Garcia shrugged. "Just an average day."

Abby sighed and looked down at the tiled floor.

"Out with it," he said.

"Suppose you saw somebody doing something . . ."

"Committing a crime?"

"Well, you weren't sure, say," Potsie broke in.

"All right."

"What would you do?"

"Investigate," said Garcia. "Check him out." He tossed a rolled-up piece of paper at them. "Or her."

"Would you come right out and ask?" Abby said.

Garcia shook his head. "No, I'd wait. I'd give him time to clear himself . . . or get himself in so deep that, zappo, I'd have him." He snapped his fingers. "Off to jail."

Abby glanced out the window. This whole thing was a waste of time. She wasn't getting anywhere.

"Look at this," he said. He pushed a piece of paper over to her. "Fingerprints. We lifted them right off an envelope."

She and Potsie bent over, bumping heads. "Sorry," they told each other.

Garcia picked up a magnifying glass. "Look at your own fingers. You can see little lines . . . ridge lines. If you look really close you can see the lines have holes in them. That's where the perspiration comes from. And that perspiration plus oil makes the fingerprint."

He handed her the magnifying glass. "Take a look."

Abby looked down at her hand. She could see exactly what he was talking about.

Potsie stared at her fingers too. "My hands are always gooey. I must leave a lot of fingerprints around."

Garcia smiled. "Suppose you leave your print on something. It's hard to see. So we have to do something to make it clear. If the print is on something dark, we dust it with light powder. If it's on something white, we have to use dark powder."

"You used dark powder on the envelope?"

_____

61

"Right," Garcia said. "I took an ordinary water-color brush, put it into a capful of powder, and brushed it lightly on the print. Nothing to it." He snapped his fingers.

"Now, this print belongs to the runaway. I made a bunch of copies and—"

Just then Witkowski said good-bye and hung up the phone. He'd be asking them a whole bunch of questions about yesterday, Abby thought. She saw his mouth open.

She stood up. "Got to go," she said nudging Potsie. "Come on." She turned to Garcia. "Can I keep the paper with the runaway's prints?"

"Why not?" Garcia said.

"Wait a minute," said Witkowski. "Don't give them that stuff. I want to find out what they've been up to."

Garcia grinned. "Relax, Witkowski. Leave the kids alone."

"I just want to study fingerprints," Abby said, grabbing the paper. "That's all."

Witkowski shook his head, muttering. "Kids have nothing to do but call here. Have to run around all over the place looking—"

Garcia pushed a book toward them. "Borrow this too. It'll tell you all about fingerprints." He leaned over to smile at them. "I wish you two looked happier."

Abby tried to smile back at him. Potsie had a sickly grin on her face.

Abby pushed the fingerprint paper into her pocket, feeling the dollar bills Lulu's grandmother had given her yesterday. She slapped the other pocket.

The ball and chain was gone.

Where?

She tried to remember what she had done with it.

With the book in her hand she hurried out the squad-room door ahead of Potsie. She could feel a lump beginning in her throat. It hurt to swallow. It was horrible to think that Garcia was a spy.

"That Garcia is just great," Potsie said looking back at the station house.

Abby closed her eyes for a moment. "I know," she said. "I just wish he had told us what he was doing yesterday. I just wish I knew for sure that he wasn't . . ."

"A spy?" Potsie asked, pulling at her pink glass necklace.

"Exactly," said Abby.

FROM THE MEMO OF ABBY JONES
FINGERPRINT FINDER

Sat. aft. after lnch.

From Garcia's bk on fgrprnting.
To find print on white thing . . . use chalk dust, or face powdr
To find print on drk thing . . . use pencil tips grnd up.

Nxt:
  Cover with Scotch tape . . . stick on card.

DID THIS:
  Worked on stuff Potsie and I stuck our prints on
  . . . like: mirror, dresser top.

DID NOT WRK ON PINK PIECE OF PAPER.
TOO BAD.
MIGHT HAVE SOLVED CRME.

CHAPTER 9

Potsie sank down on Abby's bedroom floor. "Enough of this fingerprinting," she said. "Let's do something else."

"You're right," Abby said. She shoved everything into her bottom drawer. "Let's go over to Washington Avenue and see what's happening."

"Not that spy stuff again."

"Nothing can happen to you on Washington Avenue, Pots. The whole world is walking around there. Taxicabs, cars, people . . ."

Potsie sighed. "All right. But just for a little while."

The weirdo kid, Sam, was standing in front of 222 Washington Avenue slamming a ball against the apartment building.

Abby and Potsie looked at each other. "That drip again," Potsie said.

"I meant to tell you," said Abby. "Tillie says he's crazy about her. Follows her everywhere."

"I'd hate to have a nerd like that follow me around."

"Tillie loves it. I think she has a crush on him, too, otherwise she'd tell him to get lost." She circled around him. "Have you seen Tillie?"

He threw the ball . . . "The only girl I see is a skinny little witch" . . . and threw it again. He glanced at Potsie. "And her friend the scarecrow."

Abby reached in front of him and grabbed the ball as he threw it again.

"Hey," he yelled. "Give it back, pumpkin face."

She and Potsie dashed down the street with the ball in her hand. "That miserable kid," she said to Potsie.

When they reached the front door of 214 Washington Avenue, Abby swiveled around to throw the ball back at him.

She collided with Lulu's grandmother.

"Sorry," she gasped, then grinned as she saw the weirdo kid scrambling all over the street for the ball.

"I'm so glad to see you," Lulu's grandmother said. "I was thinking that since you like to make money, maybe you'd do me a favor. Lulu and me, that is."

"Lulu?"

"I have to go out tonight, and . . ." She shook her head. "Can you imagine if I left her for a minute?" She stopped to take a breath. "Call me Nana."

Abby nodded. "Where is she now?"

"Eddie, the doorman, bless his soul. He's chasing her up and down the lobby."

Abby nodded again, watching Sam, the weirdo kid, out of the corner of her eye.

"The thing is, I thought maybe you'd baby-sit . . . you and your friend . . . just for an hour or so."

Abby looked at Potsie. Terrific. It would give them a good excuse to be in the apartment house tonight, a good excuse to be on the seventh floor. "We'll do it," she said. "Sure we will."

Potsie opened her mouth. "I guess so."

"You know where my apartment is, don't you, dear?"

"Seven something."

"Seven L," Nana said. "*L* for Lulu."

"What time?"

"Seven. Seventh floor, seven o'clock."

Abby rubbed at her arm. "Have you seen another kid around? A girl with black hair, curly, all over her head, and blue eyes?"

A line appeared between the woman's eyebrows. "I certainly have. A very annoying thing. She's always lurking around, spying on people."

"Tillie." Abby shook her head. "No, it's probably Tootsie. She's training to be a runner for the Olympics."

"She's training to be the world's greatest buttin-sky."

Just then Abby saw a reflection behind the door. Dark hair. Tillie or Tootsie, for sure.

"I have to go back now," Nana said, "before Eddie is totally worn out."

"All right." Abby moved closer to the door.

68

From inside the girl waved.

"That's Tillie?" Potsie asked.

Abby nodded. "Hey, Tillie. Come meet my friend Potsie."

Tillie came toward them. She stuck her hand out. "Want to come for dinner tonight? Potsie's coming too."

"I am?" Potsie said.

"Sorry," said Abby. "Forgot to ask."

"How soon?" Tillie asked.

"Now."

"Terrific."

"We're having chicken and—"

"I eat anything," Tillie cut in.

"We have to hurry, though," Abby said. "Potsie and I are baby-sitting . . . Lulu-sitting . . . as soon as supper's over."

"That gross kid," Tillie said. "Always screaming."

"Sticky too."

They went down the street, turned the corner, and jogged the three blocks to Abby's apartment building.

"Just in time," her mother said, and handed Abby the knives and forks, Potsie the plates. "Glad you're here," she told them, grinning. "I can always use some extra help." She handed a pile of paper napkins to Tillie. "Just put these around."

Potsie slid the plates on the table. "Oops," she said. "Forgot to call my mother."

"Go ahead," Abby said. She looked at Tillie. "Hey.

You forgot to tell your mother about eating over here too."

Tillie's face reddened. "It's all right."

"No, it's not," said Abby's mother. "I'd have a fit if I didn't know where Abby was at dinnertime."

"I didn't want to tell Abby," Tillie said slowly. "I ate before. My mother works at night, so we eat around five."

Abby's mother grinned at her. "Good girl. I like to see people who eat."

Abby grinned too. "You'll love the chicken and biscuits anyway." She turned to her mother. "I've got a baby-sitting job over at Two fourteen Washington Avenue tonight. Potsie and I."

Her mother nodded. "Good. Not too late, though."

Abby turned as the door slammed, and Dan and her father came in. For a moment everyone talked at once. Abby tried to introduce Tillie. Her father was telling her mother about a car he had sold. Dan was teasing Potsie about something. Finally they sat down and began to eat.

Abby watched Tillie from under her eyelashes. For someone who'd already had supper, she certainly could eat! Two biscuits disappeared into her mouth, and then a third.

Dan put his fork down. "That crazy Kiki Krumback is having a Halloween party tomorrow night," he said. "She invited me and Kevin."

"Kevin and me," his mother cut in.

"That reminds me," Abby told Tillie. "You're invited. Your sister Tootsie too."

Tootsie hesitated. "I'll come, but probably not Tootsie."

"Right, more girls. That's all I need," said Dan. "If Kiki thinks she's going to have a party with only two boys . . ."

"Don't be silly," Abby's mother said. "Kiki may have invited only a couple of boys, but her mother and father have invited dozens of people. Most of the neighborhood will be there."

Abby looked down at her plate. Tomorrow was Sunday. Most of the stores were closed. And she was Lulu-sitting tonight. How could she get a costume?

"What about a costume?" Tillie asked.

"You must have read my mind," Abby said.

"Go as yourself," Dan said. "A skeleton." He started to cackle.

"I'm not that skinny," Abby said.

"That's enough, Dan," her father cut in at the same time.

"I'm going to be a gorilla," said Potsie. "My mother is making me some fur legs out of an old jacket."

"Last year Tootsie went to a school party as a peacock," Tillie said. "She made the costume herself. She's as smart as a whip."

Abby sighed. She could never make a costume. And she certainly wasn't going to wear that cat costume that was hanging around in the bottom of her closet somewhere.

She wiped her mouth with her napkin and slid back her chair. "We've got to get going. Potsie and I have to baby-sit."

"You have to dish-sit, you mean," Dan said.

Abby drew in her breath. "I forgot. Listen, Dan, I promised a lady I'd take care of her granddaughter. Could you . . ."

"Not on your life," Dan said.

Abby made a face at him. She grabbed her plate and Tillie's, then Potsie stood up and took the knives and forks. They rushed into the kitchen.

By the time they were ready to leave, it was five after seven. They hurried down the street.

"I'm going to leave you here," Tillie said when they reached the corner of Washington Avenue.

"Why don't you come too? Got something better to do?"

Tillie looked uncomfortable. "I just remembered. I have to see Tootsie about something."

Abby and Potsie stood there a moment watching her as she started in the opposite direction and disappeared around the corner.

Abby shrugged. "Come on. Let's go."

Out of breath, they reached the apartment house, nodded at the doorman, and raced for the elevator.

It was going to be horrendous baby-sitting for Lulu, Abby thought. She slapped at her pockets. Too bad she had lost her ball and chain. It would have been fun to try to hypnotize her. Maybe she'd take her fingerprints instead.

The elevator door opened and they stepped out into the hall.

CHAPTER 10

She nudged Potsie. "There's the spy's apartment. Right down there."

Potsie shuddered. "Why do you always get us into this stuff? I remember when we solved the Loretta P. Sweeny mystery, I was locked in the balcony of that theater for hours, waiting for the killer to strike. Horrible."

"Don't worry," Abby said. "We're perfectly safe."

"I hope so," Potsie said. "I'm going to spend the night reading *Alone in the Dark*. I don't want to be scared more than usual."

Abby leaned on the doorbell to apartment 7L for Lulu. The door swung open.

They blinked. The entire apartment was pink: the walls, the rugs, the furniture, the curtains. And Nana was wearing a pink coat too. Next to her Abby could see Potsie was beginning to giggle. Abby cleared her throat to cover the noise of it.

"Come in, come in," Nana told them. "I almost

thought you had forgotten. I was so worried—" She broke off, looking down. Lulu was pulling at her coat.

"Want to come."

Nana sighed. "Stay here with . . . what are your names again?"

"Want to come," Lulu screamed.

Abby unbuttoned her jacket and shrugged out of it. "Abby. Abby Jones. This is Potsie."

"All you have to do is play with Lulu a little while. Then put her to b-e-d, and she'll be out like a l-i-g-h-t before I get back, I hope."

"All right," Abby said as Potsie bent over to say hello to Lulu.

"You can watch a little television, see what's in the refrigerator, do whatever you want," Nana said. She waved a pink glove in the air and went out the apartment door. "Back in an hour."

Lulu threw herself against the door. "Want to come," she screamed.

Potsie rolled her eyes at Abby. She sank down on a pink chair and opened her book. "Come on, Lulu, Potsie will read to you."

Abby laid her jacket across the other pink chair and sank down on one end of the couch, covering her ears.

A moment later Lulu was up next to her, reaching into her jacket pocket.

"Hey, what are you doing?"

"Candee?"

Abby shook her head as Lulu pulled out a bunch of stuff from her pocket. "Sorry, I don't have any."

"I have some," Potsie said. "Tic Tacs." She held out her box to Lulu.

Lulu stopped screaming. She stuffed her mouth with the little white candies.

"Now what?" Abby said. "Oh, yes. Fingerprints. Look, Lulu. I'll show you." She looked around for something to use. "Let's see what's in the kitchen."

Lulu followed her inside and pointed to the cabinet. "No," Abby said. "Maybe a glass." She reached up and took one from the cabinet. "Put your fingers around this, honey."

Lulu shook her head. "No."

"Just for a minute."

She shook her head harder.

"Come on." Abby gritted her teeth and followed Lulu as she toddled into the living room and stood up on the couch.

"TV," Lulu said.

Abby rolled her eyes and snapped on the television set.

Lulu sank back down and put her thumb in her mouth. She patted the couch with her other hand. "Sit here," she said, dribbling a little.

Abby sat down next to her and closed her eyes. What a day it had been, she thought. She glanced over at Lulu. Lulu's eyes were closed too.

Abby put her head back against a cushion. She could feel herself starting to doze.

Then someone was behind her, someone chasing her, someone with dark curly hair. *It's only Tillie,* she told herself, *only Tillie.* Then she saw the scarf, red and flowing.

It wasn't Tillie. It was Tootsie. And Tillie was shouting at her. *"Tootsie can't talk, won't talk. She's a killer, a killer, a killer."*

Abby's eyes jerked open. Her mouth felt dry, her eyes gritty. She wiped her face with her fingers. Dreaming. Only dreaming. Lulu was sound asleep next to her, and Potsie's head was bobbing over her book.

Abby wondered what time it was. She slid off the couch and stumbled into the kitchen, trying to wake up.

The clock on the wall said eleven-thirty. They'd been asleep for hours. She ran her tongue over her lips. They felt dry and cracked. She needed something to drink. Maybe a Coke or a glass of milk.

She opened the refrigerator door. Inside were dozens of white plastic cups filled with mushy vegetables and dried-up soup.

She slammed the door shut.

She'd have to call her mother and father right away. They'd be wondering how she was.

The phone was hanging on the wall next to the refrigerator. She picked it up. It rang eleven times before her mother answered. "Abby, is that you?" she asked breathlessly. "I've been worried to death, standing out in the hallway waiting . . . and Potsie's mother too."

"Nana isn't home yet, Mom," Abby said. "Don't worry. We're perfectly all right."

Her mother took a deep breath. "That's a relief. It's too late for you to come home alone. When Nana gets back, call right away. Daddy will come around for you and Potsie, I'll call her mother right now."

"Good," Abby said a little uncertainly. "Sure." She wanted to say, *Tell him to come now.* She didn't want to stay one more minute in that almost empty apartment. But before she could open her mouth, her mother had said good-bye.

Abby hung up the phone and stood there for a moment. Everything was quiet.

Quiet as death, she told herself.

She went into the living room, hugging her arms to her chest. She was freezing. Maybe she should wake Potsie up. Potsie was good company. She'd—

She heard something. Footsteps outside the door?

Maybe it was Nana.

She rushed to the door and put her hand on the knob. Then something made her stop.

Nana had her own key.

She watched the door for a moment. She could hear a slithering noise. Something.

What?

She backed away from the door and stood there in the center of the room, not moving. After a moment the noise stopped.

Then there was nothing. Not a sound.

She went back and leaned her ear against the door. She wondered what Garcia would do if he were here.

She felt a little lump in her throat. Garcia, a spy. How terrible if it were true.

Garcia would open the door.

She tried to swallow. She knew he would. Any good detective would.

But then Garcia had a gun and so did the rest of the detectives in the country, and she had nothing to protect herself with.

"Wake up, Potsie," she whispered.

Potsie stirred, then settled herself more comfortably in the chair.

Abby tiptoed over to the couch and picked up Lulu. She went into the bedroom and laid her gently in her crib.

Back in the living room she looked around. There must be something she could use against a killer. Something heavy.

On the table next to the couch was a pink ceramic lamp. "Just the thing," she told herself. She yanked the plug out of the socket and picked it up. As quietly as she could she unlocked the door.

The hall was empty. Dimly lit, the walls looked shiny, almost wet, almost moving. She shivered.

There was the sound of running feet. A voice shouting.

Leaving the door open a crack, Abby dived back into the apartment.

She caught a quick glimpse of a figure as he raced down the hall toward her.

It was someone familiar, someone she knew.

It was the weirdo boy, Sam. What was he doing here?

He threw something toward the open door, something hard and black.

A bomb?

She slammed the door, diving away from it, and landed on the floor in front of the couch.

Then more footsteps went past. Heavier, more deliberate. She raced back to the doorway in time to see the blue of a policeman's uniform disappearing after the figure.

Potsie started to wail.

"It's all right," Abby told her. "Stop. You sound like Lulu."

She looked at the object on the floor. It was only a purse. A black patent-leather purse.

She reached out and pulled it to her.

At the same time she saw the doorknob turn slowly.

"Nana?" she asked softly, gulping.

But she knew it wasn't Nana.

She backed up against the couch and held onto the pocketbook as she tried to catch her breath.

CHAPTER 11

"Let me in," the voice at the door whispered. "My key is missing. I can't find—"

From the bedroom Lulu started to cry.

Potsie was staring at Abby wide eyed.

Abby scrambled to her feet and went to the door. "Who is it?"

"André."

"André Lemonofsky?" she blurted.

"Yes. Hurry."

She backed from the door.

The knob turned again.

"Go away," Abby said, her throat so dry she could hardly get the words out.

The doorknob stopped turning. "Who is that?" the voice asked.

"Olga's in apartment seven E. E, not L," she said, her ear tight to the door. "Go there."

For a moment there was silence. Then the footsteps moved away.

Abby stepped forward to put her hand up to the knob. She could see her fingers trembling.

The spy, André Lemonofsky, had been right outside the door. She couldn't believe it.

She had to open the door. She had to take one quick look at him.

But suppose he came back? Suppose he barreled into the apartment before she could lock the door again? Or suppose he pulled out a gun or a knife?

She twisted the lock and opened the door.

"No, Abby," Potsie yelled. "Close it."

The man was standing in front of apartment 7E. As he turned slightly she saw his face. His hair was wavy, his eyes dark and sinister.

He looked like a spy. A killer. She watched him standing there. He looked impatient, nervous. He kept straightening his tie and brushing back his hair.

Then he walked quickly to the stairway, pulled open the door, and hurried away.

Abby slammed the apartment door and turned the lock.

Potsie was staring at her, hands to her mouth. "Are you crazy, Abby Jones, opening the door like that? We could have been killed, strung up by our heels like that guy in the movie—" She broke off. "Call the police."

"Witkowski? You think he would believe me . . . a second time?"

"Garcia, then."

Abby tightened her mouth. "No. We can't call Garcia. Who knows how much he's involved?"

She sighed thinking about it. "There is something, Pots. Something we should be doing. Something to help solve the case." It teased at the back of her mind. What could it be?

At last she shrugged. Lulu was going crazy in her crib.

Abby started across the room and stumbled over the black purse. In all the excitement she had almost forgotten it. She reached for it.

"Don't touch that, Abby. Who knows what's in it . . . a bomb . . . a knife . . ."

"Take a look at Lulu, will you, Potsie?" Abby asked.

As Potsie went toward the bedroom, Abbie picked up the purse and looked at it. It was a drawstring bag, jammed with stuff.

For a moment she hesitated. Her mother would have a raging fit if she knew she was opening someone's purse.

She pulled open the top of the bag and dumped everything out on the table in front of the couch.

A bunch of money, dollars, quarters, pennies. Keys. A stack of papers, a lipstick in a slim peach case, a small bottle of spray perfume.

She picked up the lipstick—Cinnamon Spice—and pulled off the top. Cool, she thought. Pale and pretty. She smeared a little on her finger, and then on her lips. Tasted good too.

It looked exactly like the lipstick Olga wore.

She reached for the perfume and sprayed both her wrists. Waving her hands around, she breathed in deeply.

Her mouth opened in a small round o.

The perfume was the same as Olga's. Same perfume. Same lipstick.

She'd bet anything this was Olga's purse.

She reached for the papers.

At the same moment a horrifying scream came from the bedroom.

Abby jumped, scattering the papers over the pink carpet.

It was Lulu, of course, playing hide and seek with Potsie. She was standing at one end of her crib, a paper in her hand; cottony stuff in her hair.

"Scared me to death," Abby said. "What's that, anyway?"

"Crib stuffing. The mattress is ripped," Potsie said.

"No, I mean the paper."

Potsie shrugged. "I didn't even notice it." She ducked down behind the crib. "I see," Lulu yelled.

Abby leaned over. She took the paper from the baby. "This is the paper with the runaway's fingerprints. The one Garcia gave us."

"Time for night-night, Lulu," Potsie said. She laid the baby down in the crib and began to pat her back. "She must have taken the paper out of your pocket."

Abby nodded and went back into the living room. She was dying to see Olga's papers.

By the time she got there, the apartment door had clicked open and Nana came in. She looked even more harried than usual. "I'm sorry," she said, "so sorry. I had to look for something, just impossible.

Your mother and father must be so worried . . . have to get someone to take you home."

Abby bent down on the living-room rug and picked up the papers. She stuffed them into the purse with the lipstick, the perfume, and the money, and tucked the purse under her arm. "My father will come for us," she said, as Potsie appeared in the hallway yawning.

Nana sank down on the couch. "That's a relief, it certainly is. So much going on . . . a policeman wandering around outside . . . all my trouble. . . ." She looked up. "And don't tell me—Lulu's up."

Abby and Potsie swiveled around. Lulu was standing in the doorway in her pajamas.

"I didn't even know she could climb out of her crib," Nana said.

"I don't know where she got that candy either," Abby said, looking at the baby's chocolate-smeared mouth.

Nana pushed at her hair and shook her head.

Lulu reached out her hand to Abby.

"Hey," Abby said.

Dangling from Lulu's hand was Abby's ball and chain.

FROM THE MEMO OF ABBY JONES, IMPRESSIVE INVESTIGATOR

Sun. morn. 10 A.M.
ttally exsted.
didn't gt to bd till 3.

BIG BREAKTHROUGH IN TWO CASES.
1.   News about Tootsie Tanner.
2.   News about Witk.'s runaway.

P.S. Go to Olga's tody. Make sure purse is hers.

CHAPTER 12

Abby stumbled out of the bathroom yawning, and collapsed on the chair in her bedroom.

Her mind was spinning.

She looked in her memo pad for notes on the run-away.

> tall
> thin
> athletic

She checked off each one. Sam, the weirdo boy, was tall, all right. He was skinny. And he was always playing ball.

She'd have to get his fingerprints, match them up with the ones she had . . . and, bam, the case would be solved.

She ran her tongue over her freshly brushed teeth, wondering how she'd ever be able to get his prints.

Too bad she hadn't thought about fingerprints

when she saw Lemonofsky at Nana's door last night. She could have zipped right out and taken the prints off the knob.

Some detective she was.

But she had other things to think about right now. More important things.

She reached under her bed for Olga's purse. She couldn't get over what she had seen in those papers at three o'clock in the morning.

Most of it was junk. A grocery list, a ten-cents-off coupon for Sweet Dreams cold cream, a yellow laundry ticket, and the picture.

The picture.

Abby picked it up and looked at it.

It was Tootsie Tanner. Her hair was black and curly, her eyes bright blue. She was wearing a light green scarf.

How had her picture gotten into a spy's purse?

Tootsie was mixed up in this mess. She had to be. She'd been wandering around 214 Washington Avenue, sticking her nose into everybody's business. And the most interesting part was that she and Olga were never seen together.

Abby leaned her head back against the chair and rubbed at the friction burn that was healing on her arm.

What to do next? There was something. She knew there was some connection she wasn't seeing. Something with the purse. Something with the weirdo boy.

Her mother poked her head in the door. "Happy

Halloween, honey," she said. "You must be worn out, getting home so late."

Abby yawned and nodded. Then she remembered. Tonight was the party. All she had to wear was that stupid little cat costume.

She sat up straight. There was something else she could do.

She tossed on her clothes, stuck her memo pad into her back pocket, and ran for the door. For a moment she hesitated. Should she call Potsie? Potsie was probably still asleep. She shrugged.

"Back in a little while," she called over her shoulder to her mother.

She raced down the four blocks to Washington Avenue looking. Tillie wasn't in Coco's, she wasn't in the yogurt place, and she wasn't in Tannenbaum's Candy Store.

Just as Abby was about to give up, someone pulled the back of her hair.

She swiveled around. "Tillie. I've been looking all over for you."

Tillie waved pale lilac fingers at her. "What do you think? Nice, quiet, ladylike." She grinned and held out her thumbs. They were coated with black polish. "Special for Halloween."

"Listen, Tillie," Abby said. "I need a favor."

"What do you say we stop in for some yogurt, or maybe an ice cream?" Tillie said. "It'll help me think better."

"I'm in a hurry," Abby said.

Tillie raised one shoulder. "What is it?"

"I don't have a costume for tonight," Abby said, "and I remembered you said Tootsie was great at that kind of thing, getting up costumes, you know?"

Tillie hesitated. "You want Tootsie . . ."

"To give me a little help."

Tillie shook her head slowly. "I don't think—"

"Listen, Tillie. I'm absolutely desperate."

Tillie thought for a moment. "You know Tootsie doesn't talk."

"That's all right," Abby said. "You could bring her over. I could just show her stuff I have around in my closet and—"

"I'll bring her over," Tillie said. "But I can't stay. Not one minute. I have things to do, lots of things."

"It's a deal."

She stood there watching as Tillie hurried up the street.

"Half an hour," she yelled back to Abby. "And Tootsie has an appetite like a horse. You'd better feed her."

Abby took a breath. That was one thing done. Two, actually. She'd be set with her costume, and she'd have time to look Tootsie over.

Now to look for that weirdo boy, and somehow get him to put his fingerprints on something.

She circled around a pile of garbage cans and crossed the street.

She stopped dead on the other side.

What an idiot she was.

She crossed the street again, tracing her steps, and started for home.

Back in her bedroom she pulled out the purse. Idiot is right, she told herself. Too bad she'd been smearing her fingers all over the purse since last night. The boy's fingerprints would have been easy to find if she had only thought about it earlier.

She made a quick trip to her mother's bedroom to borrow some face powder and an eyeliner brush and started to work.

An hour later she was finished. She sat back. There were two different sets of fingerprints on the purse. One had to be the weirdo boy's.

Carefully she looked at the paper Garcia had given her, the paper with the runaway's prints. Neither print matched it.

She sank back against the bed.

She'd been wrong. The weirdo boy wasn't the runaway. Definitely not.

She stood up and began to gather everything together. As the doorbell rang, she shoved everything under the bed and went to open the door before Dan could get it.

Tootsie was standing there, a half-smile on her face, a brown paper bag in her hand.

Abby gulped. "You certainly look like Tillie."

Tootsie flicked a finger at her black-and-white-checked scarf. Then she held out her fingers. They didn't have a drop of nail polish on them.

"Let's go in my bedroom."

Tootsie pointed to her mouth.

"You're hungry, right? I'll get us both something."

Abby went into the kitchen, looking around. Dan

had eaten everything in sight, as usual. Finally she found a box of day-old doughnuts. She piled a bunch of them on a tray with two glasses of milk, then scurried back to Tootsie.

"Here's the problem," she told Tootsie minutes later. "I want to be different . . . special . . . not a stupid little cat or something like that."

As she spoke she kept watching Tootsie. The resemblance to Tillie was unbelievable. They both moved their hands the same way, running fingers through their hair, pushing dark curls off the backs of their necks. They certainly ate the same way, shoving food into their mouths as if they hadn't eaten for days.

At last Tootsie opened Abby's closet door and began to push a jumble of jeans, shirts, and dresses back and forth. After a moment she nodded. She dumped a pile of stuff out of the brown paper bag. She looked around, then grabbed up a pencil and paper and began to write.

FROM THE MEMO OF ABBY JONES
GREAT GUMSHOE*

Sun aft.
Tootsie gone
Cstme ready
STUPENDOUS.

Cases in progress:
1. Runaway. Fgrprts *dn't* match. Weirdo boy is *not* run-
    away. (Too bad.)
2. Spy. NOWHERE.**
3. Tootsie Tanner stll dsn't tlk. Why????

*Garcia tld me gumshoe=detective. (????)
**Get over there right away and work on.

CHAPTER 13

Clutching the patent leather purse in her hand that afternoon, Abby stepped off the elevator on the seventh floor and started down the hall. She looked back. "Come on, Potsie. Why are you walking so slowly?"

Potsie looked around nervously. "I don't want to go into that spy's apartment. Suppose there are other spies there. Suppose they jump out at us . . . torture. . . ."

"I'd give them such a karate chop—" Abby began and broke off. "Listen to that kid scream." She pointed to apartment 7L for Lulu.

"Tell you what," Potsie said. "I'll go in there, play with her awhile, give Nana a break."

Abby raised her eyebrows. "You're brave as a lion, Pots."

Potsie grinned. "I know I'm a coward." She knocked on Nana's door.

Abby continued down the hall, wondering what she'd do if Garcia was in Olga's apartment.

Olga answered the door before she had taken her hand off the bell.

Abby held out the purse.

"I can't believe it." Olga's eyes opened wide. "Great girl. Where did you ever find it?" She reached for Abby's arm. "Come in. Come in."

Abby stepped inside, glancing around. "No one's here?"

"No one. I'm alone. And soon I'll have to go back alone." Olga shook her head sadly.

"What country do you come from, anyway?" Abby cut in.

"Lithuania. But that was a long time ago when I was a little girl."

"You're going back to Lithuania?"

"Goodness, no. Only to Chicago—" Olga broke off. "Listen to that noise."

Abby grinned. "Potsie playing hide-and-seek with Lulu."

"That child," said Olga, smiling. "I never heard a louder one. She certainly has her poor grandmother crazy."

"She had me crazy last night," Abby said.

"If only her father could come back. . . ." Olga shook her head again.

"Where . . ." Abby began, but Olga was opening her purse.

"I want to give you some money," Olga said. "I am

so happy to have my purse back." She fished through, stopping to look at the photograph.

"I don't want any money," Abby said. "But I wanted to ask you about—"

"Don't be foolish," Olga said. "How did you ever know it was mine?"

"Your perfume," Abby said. "Your lipstick."

"You're some detective," Olga said. "It was a terrible experience. I had left the door open a little—I don't know why—and suddenly a hand reached in. Horrible. The next thing I knew the purse was gone off the table. . . . I shut the door so fast, you wouldn't believe it."

"I saw a policeman chasing him," Abby said.

Olga nodded. "The man in the next apartment, Officer Nielson, was just going to work. He saw the thief running."

"The girl in the picture—" Abby began.

The telephone rang. Olga held out a couple of dollars. "At least take this. Have an ice cream or something." She turned and went to the phone.

Abby stood there. She wasn't going to leave until she had asked about the photo. She just had to find out Tootsie's connection to this whole spy case.

As Olga spoke into the phone, there was a knock at the door. Abby looked around wildly.

It was Garcia. She just knew it.

There was no place to hide.

She dived for an inside doorway. "I have to go to the bathroom," she whispered loudly to Olga.

Olga turned around. "Want to get the door?"

"Can't," Abby said. "Can't wait." She rushed down the hall and shut the bathroom door behind her.

She stood there panting, listening against the door. She heard Olga put the phone down and go to the apartment door.

Abby could hear it opening, and then the sound of voices. They were too low for her to hear what they were saying.

She sighed. She'd stay in there forever if she had to.

She picked up the bathroom glass—a blue plastic one with yellow flowers—and put her ear against it on the bathroom door. It was a trick she had learned from Garcia to magnify sound.

The sounds were magnified, but only a little. She could distinguish Olga's voice clearly. The other voice didn't sound like Garcia's. It sounded more like a woman's. More like . . . Whose?

She shook her head, frustrated, wondering if she should open the door.

She looked around the bathroom. A pretty room, all in blue and peach. A small blue makeup case rested on the edge of the sink. A pair of initials were embroidered on the side.

Abby picked up the case and stared at them.

T.T.

T.T. for Tillie Tanner?

T.T. for Tootsie Tanner?

Was that possible?

She stood there a little longer, then opened the door cautiously.

She was going to find out about Toostie once and for all.

Olga was back on the phone and no one was at the door anymore.

Abby sank down on a chair and waited. She wondered who Olga was talking to? Maybe to André Lemonofsky, the spy. Maybe to Garcia.

"To the party?" Olga was saying. "How nice. I'd love to bring him. He's an old friend. We went to school together."

She hung up the phone and smiled at Abby. "Are you still here? I thought you'd be getting ready for Halloween. A party or something."

"I'm all set," Abby said. "Costume's laid out on my bed."

"Wonderful," Olga said. "Maybe you could do me a favor, then. I have to go out. I need a little something at Tannenbaum's. A mask."

"Sure," Abby said. "But I wanted to ask you—"

Olga started for the kitchen. "Just go down to Lulu's grandmother. She's looking for some sugar. I told her I'd send it down as soon as I got off the phone."

"That was Lulu's grandmother at the door a minute ago?"

"Right." Olga handed her the sugar. "Tell her Terri said good luck with the recipe."

Abby nodded. "Who's Terri?"

"Me."

"You?"

"Teresa, really. But everyone calls me Terri."

"Terri." Abby repeated.

Terri walked her to the door. "You're really an angel to bring me my purse. If you won't take a reward, I'll have to find another way to make it up to you."

"Don't worry," Abby said absently. She opened the door and shut it behind her.

She walked slowly down the hall.

Halfway there she stopped. Wait till Potsie heard. She jumped up into the air, careful not to spill the sugar. If Olga was Terri, then Garcia wasn't a spy.

Sun. ltle latr.

1. Saw weirdo boy on Wash. Aven. Called Garcia.
   Garcia clled him in fr questioning.
     Boy admitted stealing purse.
     Sd he had to. Was doing for a friend.

GARCIA SAID GOOD WK.

CHAPTER 14

That night Abby followed Potsie down the steps, giggling. Potsie was dressed in tan fake fur pants and her huge gorilla head.

Abby straightened her own punk rock wig, pulled at the shirt Tootsie had made out of a couple of her old tops, and rubbed her lips with green lipstick.

Potsie sank down on the landing. "Before we go into Kiki's, let me get my breath." She lifted the gorilla head a little.

Abby sat down next to her. "If only I could figure out this whole crime . . . find Lemonofsky. . . ."

Potsie reached under the head and wiped her face. "Hot in here . . . hot as a summer day." She broke off. "I don't understand this crime. There's Tillie, and Tootsie who won't talk. There's Terri who used to be Olga. . . . Where's Olga? . . . Garcia who used to be a spy, but turned out to be a detective." She sighed. "It's just too confusing."

"You're right," Abby said. "There's a lot of threads

to this. Just what I like. A nice juicy confusing mystery."

They stood up and opened the door to the hallway. Kiki Krumback's apartment was a madhouse. People jammed the living room and spilled out into the hallway.

Abby and Potsie threaded their way past Kevin Delio in a Frankenstein mask, then stopped to say hello to Kiki. Dressed in a dotted fur costume, Kiki looked like a fat leopard.

Even Abby's brother Dan was there. He was dressed as some kind of freak.

"What are you supposed to be?" she asked.

"I was just going to ask you the same question," he said. "I'm a punk rocker."

She stuck out her tongue, then went with Potsie to the food table. Her mouth was watering.

She grabbed a plate and filled it with ziti and lasagna, and a pile of Italian bread and butter. Next to her Potsie raised her mask and reached for an onion roll.

As they ate, Abby listened to the music coming from the stereo. It was that old-fashioned kind. . . . She waved at Dan's old friend Holly Monk, who was wearing a rainbow costume, then watched some of the older people dancing. Kiki's mother was dressed as some kind of princess and Mr. Tannenbaum was a pumpkin.

Abby nudged Potsie. "Do you see Tillie and Tootsie?"

Potsie raised one furry shoulder. "So many people in masks. I don't know."

Abby reached for more butter and bumped into someone. It was Terri, wearing a black leotard and a feathered mask.

"You look terrific," Abby said. "Beautiful. I didn't know you were coming."

"Mrs. Krumback is a friend of mine from years ago," Terri said. She reached out and touched Abby's hair. "How cute you look. Too bad Lulu couldn't see you."

Abby grinned at her. "Just as well."

"Olga would love the way you look too," said Terri.

"Olga?" Abby repeated.

"Olga?" Potsie said behind her mask.

Someone tapped Abby on the shoulder. "How are my favorite girls?"

Abby could see it was Garcia, even though he was wearing a ski mask and looked like a bank robber. "Good," she said.

"How do you know each other?" Potsie asked Garcia, as she pointed to Terri.

"Went to high school together," Garcia said.

Terri nodded. "In fact he came to my apartment Friday and showed me an old autograph book." She looked at Garcia. "You and your partner have been so kind to me since—"

"Wait a minute," Abby said. "I want to ask you about Olga."

"Lulu's grandmother?"

"Good grief," said Potsie. "I was right in that apartment with a spy."

Abby stepped back. "Nana is Olga?"

"A spy," Potsie said.

"Don't be silly," Terri said. "Olga's not a spy and neither is André. Somehow the film was lost. If only they could find it, they could prove—"

"He didn't give the film to a foreign power?"

Terri shook her head. "André and Olga have been looking all over the city for it. Even Lulu's mother, Margaret, went to Washington to see if she could clear André's name somehow."

Abby nodded slowly, thinking. Her eye caught someone coming in the door. Someone with one black curl escaping from under a bird mask which covered her entire face. A red scarf was tucked around her neck.

It was Tootsie, all right. She wondered where Tillie was.

"Excuse me for just a minute," Abby said, and went toward the door. "Is that you, Tillie?"

No answer. The figure shook her head and led the way to the table.

The figure turned and nodded.

As they reached the table, Abby looked around for Garcia and Terri. They were dancing in the center of the room, while Potsie danced around by herself.

She turned back and began to fill another plate. Mrs. Krumback made the best ziti in the world.

It looked as if Tootsie thought so too. She had lifted

the bird mask a little and was stuffing her mouth with it.

Just then the red scarf slipped. Abby stared at her neck.

There was no mark, no beauty mark at all.

Abby took a bite of the ziti absently. Why did Tootsie bother to wear a scarf? It was ridiculous.

Slowly she put the plate down. Where was Tootsie when Tillie was around? Where was Tillie when Tootsie showed up?

She had never seen them together. Not once this whole weekend. Why?

She stared at Tootsie. At the same time Tootsie was turning toward the dance floor.

Tootsie jumped.

Abby tried to see why.

Then Tootsie barreled out of the room.

What had Tootsie seen?

Kevin Delio was dancing with Holly Monk. Mrs. Krumback was dancing with Mr. Tannenbaum. Garcia and Terri were there, too, twirling around laughing.

Why? Abby's mouth opened. She remembered Tootsie's photograph in Terri's patent leather purse. How could she have forgotten?

She stood there thinking . . . watching Terri dancing . . . trying to figure it out. Tootsie hadn't expected to see Terri at the party. And she didn't want Terri to see her.

Again why?

Abby threaded her way around a tall man wearing

a pirate's suit, and followed Tootsie out the door. She stopped. Witkowski's orange hair was hanging out from under his pirate's hat.

Witkowski.

Something tugged at her mind. Something to do with a case. Something . . .

And then she knew. She raced to catch up with Tootsie.

Tootsie wasn't in the hall, she wasn't on the stairway.

Abby took the stairs two at a time. "Wait up, Tootsie," she shouted. "Tillie."

She caught up with her in the lobby. "Come on back," she told Tootsie, hand on her arm. "I'll bet Mrs. Krumback is going to have cake. She had a stupendous one last year. Orange, black cats all over the top of it."

Tootsie shook her head.

"Listen," Abby said. "I know why you don't talk."

Tootsie's mouth opened.

Abby reached for her fingers. "Let me see your thumb."

Tootsie pushed her hands behind her back.

Abby grabbed for her, and held out her thumb. "Traces of black. It's hard to get that nail polish off. I tried it one time." She looked up. "Is your name Tootsie or Tillie?"

"Tootsie." She shoved the bird's mask back. "Whew, that's hot." She grinned. "There is no Tillie. I made the whole thing up. I thought you'd be mad about that business in the hall, running you down, grabbing the paper."

"And so the next time you saw me . . ."

"I had to tell you it was somebody else. So I thought of the name Tillie. Everyone in my family has a name that begins with *T*. My mother is Tonia. My father is Tex. . . ."

"And your aunt is . . ."

"Terri."

"You're the runaway," Abby said.

Tootsie sat down on the stairs. "How did you guess?"

"Just now when I saw Witkowski. I remembered they were working on a runaway case. And Terri said they'd been so kind to her." She thought for a moment. "You were always hungry, always wandering around."

Tootsie sighed. "Wandering around trying not to run into Aunt Terri and still keep an eye on her to make sure she didn't find me."

"But what was the paper? The pink piece of paper?"

"Here's the way it went," Tootsie said. "When I was a little girl we lived on Washington Avenue. Aunt Terri, my parents, me. I loved it. I always wanted to come back. One day I ran away from Chicago, took a train, and landed up right here."

"Your aunt came to look for you."

"Yes. My mother has four other children. Aunt Terri wasn't married, she had vacation. They guessed I might come here."

"So Terri came back to your old apartment. . . ."

"Yes, the super lent it to her."

"But the pink paper?" Abby asked, remembering the friction burn.

"It was a letter from my mother to Aunt Terri. I recognized the writing. I wanted to see what she had to say."

Abby nodded. "How about—"

"Going back?" Tootsie nodded. "I'm getting lonesome for my brothers, sick of sleeping in the basement at Two fourteen Washington Avenue, sick of being hungry." She stood up.

"Hey, one more thing. That weirdo kid, Sam . . ."

Tootsie rolled her eyes. "The purse. I know. I have to straighten out that whole thing. Try to get him out of trouble. I was desperate for money. I knew Aunt Terri wouldn't mind if she knew it was for me. I asked him to get it for me." She shrugged. "When the policeman came after him he threw it into an apartment."

Abby grinned. "Right into my hands."

Abby followed Tootsie back into Kiki's apartment and tapped Witkowski on the back. "Guess who I found?"

"Who?" said Witkowski, his mouth wrapped around a hero sandwich.

"Your runaway."

Too bad, she thought as she grinned at him, that she hadn't used the ball and chain to hypnotize Tootsie. She might have solved the case a lot sooner.

Then she slapped her forehead.

The ball and chain.

Good grief.

She looked over to where Tootsie and her aunt Terri were hugging in the middle of the floor.

Garcia winked at her and put his fingers in a V-for-victory sign.

She grabbed Potsie's arm. "Come with me," she said.

Halfway out the door she turned back and shouted to Garcia. "We'll be right back. Save us a piece of cake."

CHAPTER 15

Abby raced down the street, dragging Potsie behind her. People on the street stopped to stare at them.

"Catch that crazy gorilla," some boy yelled.

"Stop, Abby," Potsie yelled. "Stop this minute. I don't know one thing that's going on. Where are we going?"

"Going?" Abby repeated. "Going? To Olga Lemonofsky's apartment."

"To Nana's? Why—"

"To solve the spy mystery, of course," she said breathlessly.

"Of course," Potsie muttered. "Of course."

They rushed past the doorman, who yawned when he saw them. Then he sat up straight. "Hey," he yelled. "Who are you? Where—"

It was too late. The elevator door opened and they scrambled inside.

Abby punched the button for the seventh floor and leaned back against the wall.

"Tell me," Potsie began.

"There's no Tillie," Abby said, "to begin with. There's only Tootsie. She ran away from Chicago and came here. Her aunt came looking for her."

Potsie bobbed her head up and down, lips moving. "Got it. But what has that got to do with the spy?"

"Nothing, really. It just made me remember the ball and chain . . . and the chocolate candy—" She broke off. "Don't you see, Pots?"

"I certainly do not see," Potsie said, stamping one furry foot. "I certainly don't see anything. That's been happening to me all weekend."

The elevator door slid open and they stepped out into the eggplant hall.

"In a few minutes," Abby said. "Cross your fingers that I'm right. If I am, André can come home, and everything will be all right for the Lemonofskys."

She pounded on the door to 7L for Lulu.

A moment later Nana opened it. Her eyes widened. She began to scream.

"It's only me," Potsie said. "I'm not a gorilla."

Nana stepped backward and sank onto the couch. "You two scared the wits out of me. I never even recognized you."

Just then Lulu appeared in the doorway, her mouth covered with chocolate. She gurgled when she saw Potsie, and started to laugh.

"Where does she get that candy? I have it hidden away. At least I think . . ." Nana said, her voice trailing off.

"You're missing a roll of film," Abby broke in.

Nana looked sad. "The film, yes."

"André's missing his key."

"Is he?"

"Yes," Potsie said. "Even I know that."

"I was missing my ball and chain," Abby said.

"Good grief," said Potsie. "This could go on all night. Get to the point, will you?"

"I am," said Abby. "I am." She turned to Nana. "Where did you hide the chocolate?"

"In the cabinet, behind the cereal."

"I'll bet that's gone too. And I know where she's hiding the stuff."

"How could you possibly—"

"Let's go into Lulu's bedroom," Abby said.

Potsie pulled off her gorilla mask. "I can't stand this thing one more minute."

Lulu trotted over to the couch and began to rub the gorilla fur, as Abby led the way into the bedroom. "The only thing is," Abby said, "we may have to pull this whole mattress apart."

Nana frowned. "That's what the baby does. All the time. Pieces of stuffing all over the place. In her hair, her clothes."

Abby reached into the crib and dragged out the mattress. "Sticky," she said.

"Lollipop," said Nana. "Orange."

Abby closed her eyes. She ran her fingers along the side of the sticky mattress until she found the opening she was looking for. "You see," she said, reaching inside. "This is the perfect place to hide things. I should have realized last night when I was baby-sitting."

Nana's eyes widened. "You don't suppose . . ."

"I do suppose." Abby reached in deeper, pulling out wads of stuffing. She felt her hands graze against something cold and sharp. She jumped.

"What's the matter?" Potsie said from the door-way.

"Something . . ." Abby looked up . . . "just felt odd for the moment." She reached in again and wrapped her fingers around the cold object. She began to grin as she pulled it out and dangled the key ring in her fingers.

"Keys," said Nana. "André's keys."

"Yes," said Abby. "There's more here too." She pulled out some more stuffing, then one by one laid the rest of the objects on the floor next to the crib. Two candy bars, one comb, Potsie's pink glass neck-lace, a red scarf—probably Tootsie's, Abby thought—and a small roll of X90 color film.

"I have to sit down," Nana said. "I can't believe it."

"My necklace," Potsie said. "Good grief. I didn't even know it was missing."

Just then Lulu appeared in the doorway. She had on Potsie's gorilla mask and her hands were covered with Abby's green punk lipstick.

Abby and Potsie looked at each other. "Let's bring her back to the party," they said.

"Wonderful," said Nana. "I've got to go out and

find André. Tell him he can come home. Call Washington for my daughter-in-law."

Abby reached for one of Lulu's sticky hands. "Hurry, Pots. We don't want to miss the Halloween cake."

Sun. night. oops Mon. morn.

Party's over.
Case solved.

Met André Lemonofsky. (Nana brought him to party to give film to Garcia.) Not so sinister after all.

Things to do tomorrow:
1. Find mystery.
2. Murder kind/or spy.
3. Solve.

**Good grief. Have to do my homework.

SPY STORY SOLVED

According to Detective James Garcia a major spy story was solved when Abigail Jones, Junior Detective, discovered a roll of film tucked inside a ripped crib mattress.

Ms. Jones said that Lulu, the baby daughter of André Lemonofsky, often took things and hid them, so it was logical for her to have taken the film from her father's pocket.

Mr. André Lemonofsky was reunited with his family. He has been cleared of all charges.

When photographers took Ms. Jones's photo with her friend Penelope Olivia Torres, she made the following statement: "This is not the first time I've solved a crime. . . . It won't be the last."